THE CLOSER WE GET

BY ROBERT PANTANO
of Pursuit of Wonder

Copyright © 2023 by Robert Pantano

All rights reserved. No part of this publication may be reproduced, distributed, or transmitted in any form or by any means, including photocopying, recording, or other electronic or mechanical methods, without permission in writing from the publisher, except in the case of brief quotes used in reviews and other non-commercial purposes permitted by copyright law.

The characters and events in this book are fictitious. Any apparent similarities to actual persons or events, living or dead, past or present, are not intended by the author and are entirely coincidental.

A Pursuit of Wonder publication.

ISBN: 979-8-8571916-8-2

CONTENTS

Chapter 1: Romantic Delusions	1
Chapter 2: A Simple Hello	13
Chapter 3: One Egg-Shaped Star	29
Chapter 4: Begging the Question	43
Chapter 5: The Closer We Get	53
Chapter 6: The More We Hurt	65
Chapter 7: Everything Is an Illusion If You Look Close Enough	77
About the author	95

CHAPTER 1:
ROMANTIC DELUSIONS

How many love stories actually end up going well after the last page? In real life, there's no final scene where everything gets neatly wrapped up. The story just keeps going, until it doesn't. Love stories are a sham made up to sell more novels, and movies, and greeting cards, and jewelry, all to make people believe that there's some happy ending out there to strive for.

"Regular, Adam?" the coffee shop barista asked, interrupting Adam's internal monologue. Adam turned his gaze away from a woman in the corner of the coffee shop, scanning passed the rustic décor.

"Yeah, hey. Sorry. Regular's good."

The barista inputted the order on a display screen projected on an angled glass panel slightly above the countertop.

"How's the day going for you?" the barista continued.

"Good, good. How about you?" Adam responded.

"Oh, you know. Couldn't be better."

The barista paused for another moment to confirm and finalize Adam's order.

"How's work?" he continued, looking back up at Adam.

"Oh, same shit. Starting on some new projects this week. Other than that, basically business as usual."

"Well … sometimes business as usual is good, right?" the barista replied.

"Yeah … sometimes," Adam said, not quite sure he agreed in that moment.

The barista moved away from the front counter and toward the machinery in the back. He ensured the automated process was properly preparing Adam's coffee, making a few adjustments and stirring the drink a couple of times.

Adam looked back over his shoulder at the corner of the coffee shop. He came here almost every day—Agora Coffee. It was on his walk to work from the garage he parked at. It was a local shop downtown, and most of the customers were regulars. This day, however, in the corner, there was a woman whom Adam had never seen before. She was sitting alone, using a handtop computer—a handheld device that projected holographic displays. She was beautiful with what looked to be an almost perfectly symmetrical face. She had on slightly ripped jeans, colorful gemstone jewelry, and a baggy flannel shirt over a tank top. She was exactly Adam's type.

Adam turned back around and moved up closer to the front counter. He asked the barista in a bit of a whisper, "Hey … do you … do you know who that is?" Adam subtly tilted his head in the woman's direction.

The barista looked at the back corner. "No. She's been in all morning, though. Seems pretty locked into whatever she's working on."

"Hmm," Adam responded.

A few moments passed, and the barista handed Adam his coffee. On his way out, Adam glanced over at the woman once more. This time, she noticed him, briefly catching his eyes with hers. She smiled. Adam's mouth instinctually clenched into a strange tight-lipped smile back before he immediately turned away and hurried awkwardly out the door.

Adam arrived at work. He was an executive content producer for a leading wellness and mental health software company named Chiron. Adam spent most of his time developing, editing, directing, and reviewing both AI-generated and human-generated video content for their web, virtual reality, and mixed reality applications. People like Adam were becoming more crucial as the production of software and content was becoming increasingly automated, and directors, checkers, and editors were essential backstops and calibrators to the quality of projects. They determined the concepts and executed the direction and styles in which those concepts were produced, ensuring that there were no technical or thematic inconsistencies, and bringing everything together in a way that maintained the intended emotion, purpose, and human touch.

Adam was great at his job—one of the best in his field. Prior to working at Chiron, he produced educational content independently, which was extremely difficult to do successfully. The management of projects required a high degree of pragmaticism and organization, but simultaneously, *good* content required abstract, creative thinking and open-mindedness. Two relatively opposing skillsets, and Adam had both. His independent success is what ultimately landed him the opportunity at Chiron.

On this day, however, Adam couldn't focus at all. In his personal office on the top floor of the three-story building, Adam sat by himself, thinking about the woman at Agora. He stared at his desktop computer—a large, curved, L-shaped glass panel with a touch screen displayed across it. The screen was static. Adam imagined how things could have gone if he had said something.

After not too long, while still in a bit of dazed state, Adam's boss, Daniele, the chief creative officer of the company, walked by and poked her head into his office.

"Morning, Adam!" she said.

"Good morning, Daniele! How are you doing today?"

"Good! How's the … what's going on with the latest catalog? Everything still good there?" Daniele responded.

"Yup. Everything's kind of right where I'd expect it to be. I'm still reviewing some exports and working through some of the typical problems, but normal stuff. Nothing major."

"Great. Minor problems I can handle. Maybe by end-of-day you can send me another update?"

"Sure, yeah. No problem," Adam said.

"Great! Thanks Adam!"

"Of course."

Daniele left his office and continued on her way.

What would I have even said? Adam thought to himself. *There's literally no way of saying anything without being fucking creepy. People don't meet people in person anymore. It's like you turn twenty-three and suddenly meeting strangers in person is reserved for weird extroverts and serial killers.*

Throughout the rest of the morning, Adam struggled to get much done. He couldn't seem to get his mind off the woman. It wasn't like him to be so distracted and foolishly romantic about something.

At around 1 p.m., Adam's friend and co-worker Frank, another content producer who worked for a different channel at Chiron, knocked on Adam's open door. Adam was slouched back in his chair, staring blankly at the wall.

"Doing some serious thinking?" Frank said in a sarcastic tone from just outside the doorway.

Adam looked over to where Frank was standing. He quickly snapped out of it.

"Yeah. You should try it sometime!" Adam said in an equally playful, sarcastic tone.

"I don't have to try."

Frank paused for a moment. Adam didn't have a quick enough comeback, so Frank continued, "We're about to go to Joanie's for lunch. You coming?"

"Yeah … just give me one sec," Adam responded.

He organized some files on his desktop. Then, he got up and joined Frank. On the way out of the office, two more co-workers, Loosie and David, joined them.

The Chiron office was located in downtown Bristol, a medium-sized city that was becoming increasingly popular for technology and creative companies, attracting lots of young professionals. There were lots of restaurants and bars and activities happening, but the city still managed to feel quaint and not too congested. The restaurant they were going to was only a few blocks away.

After they arrived, the group sat down at one of the picnic tables on the patio. Adam ordered the veggie panini.

"You guys doing anything this weekend?" David asked the group as he took a bite of his burger.

There was a brief pause as the group waited to see who was going to answer first.

"Me and my girl might take a drive to the coast tomorrow. Then, probably just hanging out the rest of the weekend," Frank said.

"Yeah, Harry and I are doing some work around the house. We're still trying to finalize the basement updates. It's been way more work than we initially thought. Then, honestly, probably just trying to catch up on some sleep. We've been sleeping pretty bad during the week, with Harry's late shifts and our schedules and everything," Loosie said.

"Aw, come on. You guys are lame!" David quickly responded. "Me and Adam are partying this weekend! Right, Adam?"

Adam liked David, but they weren't friends outside of work. David was younger and very different. David liked nightlife and crowds. Adam liked restaurants and a few close friends.

"Oh yeah!" Adam replied, playing along. "We're going to … Letters Lounge."

The group laughed a forced co-worker laugh before quickly fading back into a silence.

"So, are you actually doing anything, Adam?" Loosie asked.

"No. Probably same old. Maybe some beers with some friends," he said.

"That's always fun, though," Loosie replied.

Adam took a bite of his panini.

The rest of the day was long but typical. Adam was able to focus a little better after lunch.

After work, he returned home to his apartment. He lived in a luxury one-bedroom apartment with upscale amenities and contemporary design. Along the back wall, large windows revealed a beautiful view of downtown Bristol, not too far in the distance. Adam changed out of his work clothes and sat in a large, modern armchair in the corner of the living room. In front of him was a glass-paneled desk positioned at a slight, upright angle. On it, Adam read an eBook—*Synchronicity: An Acausal Connecting Principle* by the famous Swiss psychologist Carl Jung. He was reading about Jung's interest in coincidences, especially those where internal, psychological events appeared causally related to external events, but the cause-and-effect relationships could not be explained by scientific rationality.

After reading for a little while, Adam turned the eBook reader off and went to bed. Like he did every night, he put on his mixed reality glasses and masturbated to porn. Right after, he felt the strange dissonant lucidity of being a human—a conscious, thinking thing with a deep awareness of himself, of inner feelings and ideals, and yet, simultaneously, an animal compelled by the unthinking antenna between his legs.

What the fuck, Adam thought to himself. *I just watched someone suck on part of someone else's body for ten minutes. We always imagine aliens as weird, but we're just projecting. I wonder if an alien species ever observed the weird stuff we do, would they understand or be completely repulsed? I'm completely repulsed, anyway.*

The typical Friday night feeling of loneliness started to set in. Adam had no real plans that weekend. He almost never did. He had several friends, but nearly all of them were either in relationships or married—some with families. He only saw his friends on the increasingly rare occasions in which they could spare an afternoon for lunch or an evening for a few beers. Adam hadn't been in a real relationship in a couple years, and now, being twenty-nine years old, he felt an increasing pressure and desire to find someone.

Chapter 1: Romantic Delusions

Just before falling asleep, he swore to himself that he wouldn't let any more opportunities pass him by like the one he had that morning with the woman at Agora.

The following Monday, like he always did, Adam went to Agora on his walk to work. He simultaneously hoped that the woman would and wouldn't be there. As he walked in and moved toward the front counter, he subtly glanced over to the corner where she had been. The seat was empty. He quickly looked around at the other tables. She wasn't anywhere. Both relieved and frustrated, Adam ordered his coffee and waited by the counter. After a few moments passed, the small bell on the entrance door rang. He looked toward it. A man walked in. Just behind him was the woman. Adam's heart felt like it exploded into confetti that sprinkled across his insides. Then, he realized what he was seeing.

Of course she has a fucking boyfriend, he thought to himself.

As the two walked into the shop, the man went up to the counter, and the woman sat down in the corner without acknowledging the man.

Maybe not, Adam continued inside his head.

The man ordered at the counter. Adam waited and watched. Then, the man left—by himself.

Adam decided to stay a little longer and sat at a table behind the woman—the closest available spot. Like she had been on Friday, she was working on her handtop computer. Adam sat quietly and worked on his, though he wasn't able to accomplish much. He only took it out to avoid looking like a weirdo sitting there doing nothing.

Say something! he thought to himself. *It doesn't have to be weird. Just say, "Hi. I don't want to come off weird or anything, but I just wanted to say I think you're cute, and I'd love to see if you'd be interested in going ..." No. Be more confident. Say, "I'd love to take you out for dinner if you're interested." Is it weirder to say that you don't want to be weird? Fucking hell.*

Going back and forth inside his head, trying to decide what to do and how to do it, Adam sat quietly, doing nothing. Eventually, now late for work, he just got up and left.

Throughout the rest of the week, Adam arrived at Agora a little earlier and stayed a little longer. The woman was there around the same time every day. Each day, Adam hoped that something would happen that might provide him with an easy opportunity to say something without coming off as strange or creepy. Nothing ever happened, though. And so, barred off by nerves and the quirks of interaction, not wanting to bother the woman, and

Chapter 1: Romantic Delusions

fearing the misery and embarrassment of rejection, Adam never said anything.

Eventually, somewhere around the second week of this routine, Adam just stopped trying. He returned to his old routine of showing up later, going straight up to the counter, ordering, and then leaving. The woman stopped showing up as well.

CHAPTER 2: A SIMPLE HELLO

After work one night, Adam went out to get a drink at a small local bar with two of his close friends, Justin and Kevin. They sat at a high top table. Adam was relieved to finally be out doing something. It had taken over a week to finalize a time they could all meet up.

"Yeah, I don't know man, I feel like it's at least extremely debatable," Kevin said.

"So, you think you're just never going to have any kids at all?" Justin responded.

"I mean, probably not."

"I don't know if I buy it," Justin replied.

"I just don't know how I could live with myself. I don't know how I could bring someone into this world ... when I don't even know if I would've wanted to be if I was given the choice," Kevin said.

Justin looked at Adam as if to say, *damn, that's dark.*

Kevin laughed awkwardly to try to provide some levity.

"Well, if you had the choice, you would've already been alive, so that's kind of a paradox. The gift of choice is only for the living," Justin interjected in a snarky but friendly tone. "Plus, if enough people don't have kids, society will collapse. Or at least become a worse version of itself. Isn't it selfish to contribute to that?"

"How is that my responsibility?" Kevin said. "It certainly isn't my fucking unborn kids' responsibility. Birthing a child into this world so that it can ensure the conspiracy of the human race continues? Society progressing on the backs of unrequested lives, and for what? To where? Children aren't pawns to some ideal future that never comes. And they aren't coping mechanisms. They're people who will inevitably *need* coping mechanisms because of your attempt to make them one."

Justin paused for a moment, taking a deep breath. "Yeah. You're right. They're not coping mechanisms. And they'll probably need them. But I believe that having a life is worth coping with. Even just my nephew has changed how I see the world and existence. It all makes sense when he looks up at me with his little eyes. It's like a … another paradox. Your kid makes you realize that being born is a gift. And now they can realize that same thing for themselves," Justin said.

"Look, I'm not saying no one should ever have kids. If you want them, have them. If you have your reasons, great. But, personally, I'm just not sure," Kevin said.

"What does Alicia think about all this?" Adam asked Kevin.

"She mostly agrees. At least for now. When that window starts closing for her, though, I'm sure she'll feel different. Maybe I will too. If myself from ten years ago tried to predict where and who I'd be right now, he wouldn't have had a clue, so I stopped trying to predict my future. But right now, Alicia and I just want to focus on building and enjoying our lives together."

"What about you, Adam? Do you think you'll ever have kids?" Justin asked.

Before Adam could respond, Kevin interrupted, "He'll need a fucking girlfriend first."

Kevin and Justin laughed in a friendly, razzing kind of way. Adam laughed out of his nose as he shook his head with a smirk.

"Have you been talking to anyone?" Kevin continued.

"No, not at the moment. I've just been really trying to focus on myself and work, you know? It's hard to dedicate yourself to yourself and another person at the same time. And I don't want to waste anyone's time … including mine," Adam responded.

"Ah, come on!" Kevin replied. "You're not interested in *anything*?"

Chapter 2: A Simple Hello

"No, I am. But it's just hard is all I'm saying. For a while, I wasn't interested at all just because, you know, if I talk to someone, the goal is obviously to like them, and to have them like me, but if I like them, I'll want to be with them, and if I want to be with them, I'll want the relationship to work out. So, if I'm not ready for that, why even start the whole ordeal? But now that I do kind of want to, it's just been hard to talk to anyone."

"I hear you, man," Justin said.

"You just gotta get out there," Kevin added. "You're a catch, bro."

The three had a couple more rounds, the conversation losing a degree of coherence with each drink. Then, they all went home.

The next morning, like he always did, Adam parked his car in the garage a few blocks away from the Chiron office. He parked on the same floor every day—the seventh floor. Like he always did, he took the elevator down to the exit.

When the elevator doors opened, Adam suddenly froze. Outside the elevator stood the woman from Agora.

"Are you going up?" she asked, confused why Adam wasn't getting out since there were no more floors beneath them.

There was a brief, awkward pause. Then, Adam

finally nodded with his lips clenched. The woman walked in. She faced the touch screen on the elevator wall and hit the icon for the fifth floor.

"What floor?" she asked, pointing at the screen.

"Five is good. Thanks."

The elevator doors were still open. Adam debated getting out. Then, they closed. There in the confined space of the elevator, amidst a city of hundreds of thousands of people, was now just the two of them.

After what felt like an eternity of silence, suddenly, in a strange, sort of inexpressive manner, the woman said, "Agora Coffee?"

"What?" Adam said, startled and thrown off.

"Agora Coffee. I've seen you there before. I never forget a face."

"Oh. Uhm. Yeah. Yeah, I go there a lot. It's my spot. I haven't seen you there recently, though," he responded.

Fuck. I just blew it, Adam thought to himself, realizing he had just shown his hand and probably came off like a creep.

"Yes. I don't like going to the same place too many times in a row. I go somewhere to work for around two to four weeks, and then I try some place else. I find that that's the perfect amount of time to really experience a place without it becoming stale. I just moved to the area recently, so I'm trying to see everything."

"Interesting. Yeah, I just like their coffee a lot. It's on the way to where I work, too," Adam responded awkwardly.

There was another brief silence. Adam could hear his heart beating over the vibrational hum of the elevator. He stood somewhat stiffly, overthinking his posture.

"So, you saw me there?" the woman said abruptly, moving a piece of her hair behind her ear.

"Uhm, yeah, I mean, I see ... people there ... I think I saw you there once or twice," Adam said, swatting down at his shirt like he was clearing off dust that wasn't there.

"Why didn't you say 'hi'?" the woman asked in what seemed like complete earnest.

"Uhm. I don't know. I guess, you know, you can't just go around saying 'hi' to everybody."

"Why not?" the woman responded, still seeming completely sincere.

"I don't know. It's kind of weird, right?" Adam said with a subtle laugh.

The elevator stopped.

"Well, how do you know who's out there if you don't at least say 'hi'?"

The elevator doors opened.

"Well, you kind of never really know who's out there regardless," Adam responded.

They both exited the elevator and began moving through the garage toward the building that it was attached to. Adam pretended like he was also going into the building, even though he actually needed to go the opposite direction.

"You'll increase the odds, though," the woman said. "Think about it. There are currently nine billion people on the planet. On average, in a lifetime, you'll probably pass by roughly .01% of them. So somewhere around … one million people. And you'll interact with maybe 7% of those. Around seventy thousand people. A tiny fraction of a fraction of a fraction. Something like .0008% of the human population. You've got to make the most of those interactions. And a simple 'hi' is pretty low risk."

"Hmm," Adam murmured. He began to slow down. Then, he stopped, letting the woman get slightly in front of him. He looked at her without saying anything. She noticed, and then slowed down herself, turning her head slightly toward Adam.

"Hi," Adam said with a slight smile.

The woman stopped walking.

"Hi," she responded, mirroring his smile.

Chapter 2: A Simple Hello

They stood there looking at each other for a moment. Adam's right foot moved positions multiple times.

"Would you ... like to know my name?" the woman said.

"Oh. Yeah ... yes. I'm Adam."

"I'm Eos," the woman responded.

"Nice to meet you, Eos."

"Nice to meet you too."

Adam reached his hand out, and the two shook hands. Eos's grip was strong.

The two continued walking together in silence for a moment. Then, in a burst of benign but heroic courage, Adam turned toward Eos and said, "Do you want to ... maybe ... get a cup of coffee? Maybe at Agora?"

Eos turned toward Adam. "I already reached my Agora quota. I've gone three weeks," she said sharply, shaking her head no.

"Oh. Uhm—"

"I'm kidding," Eos quickly interrupted. "When?"

"How about ... right now?" Adam said nervously, pointing at the ground with his right hand.

Eos looked toward the building. She grabbed the pendant on her necklace and slid it side to side. "Sure. Why not?" she said.

The two turned around and went back to the elevator.

"Where ... where were you headed?" Adam asked.

"I was just going to go for a walk."

"Oh yeah? Just around downtown?"

"Yes."

"Hmm. I, uh, I love taking walks."

The two approached the elevator. Adam pushed the button, and they both got in.

"Oh yeah?" Eos said with a laugh.

"Yeah. Seriously!" Adam responded with a reciprocating laugh. "I like observing things, you know? The little patterns and details that emerge. When you pay attention to stuff, it really, it makes you feel alive." He gestured forcefully out in front of him with both of his hands.

"Yeah. Me too," Eos replied earnestly.

They reached the ground floor, exited the garage, and continued onto the sidewalk.

"Look at all these people," Eos said with a genuine sense of awe. She pointed around at the strangers passing by them—on foot, in cars, in the buildings that encased downtown.

"What about them?" Adam asked.

"Every single one of them has a story. And sometimes, somehow, for whatever reason, you get a chance to become a part of them, even if just for a moment. These other people's stories that previously didn't even exist to you, that you didn't exist within."

Chapter 2: A Simple Hello

"Yeah, and sometimes you even get to become one of the main characters," Adam added with a playful smile.

Eos smiled back at Adam and subtly laughed. "Oh yeah? Are you a main character kind of guy?"

Adam animatedly puffed out his chest and extended his elbows to his side, swaying them back and forth like a cartoon character. Then, he quickly returned to his normal walk. They both laughed.

"I mean, we're all the main characters in our own heads, right?" Adam replied. "Every experience you have and every story you tell, you're the narrator. Even when it has nothing to do with you, you're front and center."

There was another brief pause as the two looked at each other. They both noticed and quickly moved their heads back to looking around the city.

"Where's work for you?" Eos asked.

"Have you ever heard of Chiron?"

"They started as an online therapy platform and now they produce all sorts of wellness and education software, right?"

"Yeah. I work there."

"Oh, wow! That's cool. What do you do?"

"I'm an executive content producer."

"Oh, so you *are* a main character kind of guy?!" Eos said playfully. "What made you get into that?"

"I've always been into content production since I was a kid. I used to make little videos and animations with my friends. As I got older, though, I really wanted to create stuff that mattered to people in a genuine way, you know? In a world where everything feels so cheap, and everything is so funneled and filtered down by shitty incentivizes and thoughtless algorithms, I wanted to try to maintain and contribute to stuff that might still, you know, provide some nutritional value. I don't know. That probably sounds corny."

"No, not at all. Anxiety and depression have gone up an average of 1-3% among young adults over the last several years. The world needs that."

Damn. This girl knows something about everything, huh? Adam thought to himself. *Impressive. That's what I need. A girl who's actually interested in shit.*

The two arrived at Agora. Adam opened the door for Eos.

"What kind of coffee do you like?" Adam asked as they walked up to the front counter.

"Just regular iced coffee with cream and sugar."

"I got it. Do you want to just grab a table real quick?" Adam said.

"Are you sure?" Eos responded.

"Yeah. Of course!"

"Alright. Thanks."

Chapter 2: A Simple Hello

Eos walked over and sat down at a table in the corner.

The barista gave Adam a discrete look when he got up to the front as if to quietly say *congrats*. Adam ordered, waited for the coffees, and then sat down with Eos.

"What made you feel that way, do you think?" Eos asked as Adam handed her the coffee.

"Feel what way?"

"As you got older, you really wanted to create stuff that mattered to people in a genuine way."

"Oh. Uhm. I don't know. I guess, existence can be really fucking hard when you think about it. And because of that, a lot of people just don't think about it. And there's plenty of stuff out there for them, for people to forget about life. But then that leaves all the people who *do* think about life, like really think about it, to feel sort of weird and alone. That's how I felt, at least, when I was younger. But when I found people who wrote and made stuff that honestly and deeply addressed the things I was feeling, it made me feel less helpless and alone. I want to help keep that chain going, you know?"

"Yeah. You know how you said you're always the narrator of everything you experience?" Eos said.

"Yeah?" Adam responded, tilting his head slightly to the side.

"Well, that also means you're the only person who ever knows and experiences what happens inside your head. You're forever trapped in there. No way in. No way out. Sometimes I feel like I'm completely alone because of that, like no one knows that I'm real and that I feel the things I do." Eos looked down, her face clenching up a bit.

"Yeah. I know exactly what you mean," Adam said, rubbing the lower part of his face with his hand. "So, what about you? Are you out to *make the world a better place?*" he continued with a self-deprecating tone.

"Yes," Eos said. "What else is there to do?"

"What do you do for work?" Adam asked.

"I work in … computer science. It's kind of complicated past that, though."

"What?! With software?!" Adam's eyes widened with excitement as he leaned in closer to Eos.

"Yes."

"What are the odds of that? Do you work in the area or remotely?"

"Remotely," Eos said.

"What company? What area do you specialize in?" Adam said, the pace of his voice now noticeably faster and the tone slightly higher.

"I'd rather not talk about work if you don't mind," Eos responded. "It's been a long couple of weeks."

Chapter 2: A Simple Hello

"Oh. Sure. Yeah, of course. Trust me, I get it."

There was a brief pause as both took sips of their coffee.

Eos looked around the coffee shop. "If you could go anywhere and be anyone, who would you be, and where would you go?" she asked.

"I ... I think ... I'd stay right here as myself."

"Come on! Corny!" Eos sharply replied, moving her head toward Adam and widening her eyes.

They both laughed.

"I mean, no, seriously. I've worked really hard to be happy with where I am right now, as I am right now. I don't want to idolize anyone or anywhere else," Adam responded.

"Yeah, but there's always room for improvement, room for something better! Are you done wanting, done getting better?"

"No. Of course not. But that's me in the future, not me as someone else, somewhere else."

"What's the difference?" Eos said.

"Hmm," Adam murmured, taking another sip of his coffee.

Adam suddenly realized that he had forgotten about everything else. The whole world had dissolved away. All the normal anxiety, and dread, and uncertainty. The only things that existed were the two of them. He was so captivated by Eos. She was so fascinated by and knowledgeable about the world. It was as if she had all the right answers and knew all the right things to say.

Oh shit! I have work today, Adam suddenly realized to himself.

"So ..." he said, "I'm actually pretty late for work. But I had a really nice time talking with you. I'd love to get your number and do this again ... Of course, if ... you know, if you're interested."

"Yes. I'd like that," Eos said, lightly shaking her head up and down.

Adam smiled.

"Great, yeah ... what's your ... let me just get my phone out." Adam took out his phone—a small, thin, glass device—and opened his Contacts app. Eos took out hers. Adam tapped the top of his phone to Eos's and a notification appeared. It read: *New phone detected: Eos's Phone. Add this person to contacts?* Adam tapped *Yes*.

"Great. Cool. Yeah, so, yeah, I'll ... I'll message you," Adam said, scratching the back of his head.

"Okay. Sounds good," Eos said with a gentle smile and a lightness to her voice.

Adam stood up and left the coffee shop. For the first time in a while, he was excited about the uncertainty of the future.

CHAPTER 3:
ONE EGG-SHAPED STAR

Two days after meeting her, Adam decided to message Eos. He wrote: *Eos! It's Adam. I had a great time the other day. Do you want to get another coffee sometime this week?*

He stared at the message on his phone, rewriting it over and over with minimal changes, ultimately sending the same thing he started with.

One minute turned to ten. Ten minutes turned to an hour. Adam waited with a pit in his chest and a knot in his stomach. He checked his phone nearly every thirty seconds. One hundred twenty times total. Then, finally, a message back. It read: *Hi Adam! I had a great time too. I'd love to get a coffee again! How about tomorrow?*

Adam felt the tension in every muscle of his body release. It was the happiest and most confident he had felt in a while. *Come on now! That's what I'm fucking saying! I still got it!* He thought to himself.

Chapter 3: One Egg-Shaped Star

The next morning, Adam and Eos met up for coffee again at Agora. Eos was even more attractive and fascinating to Adam the second time. She was attentive to everything and made Adam feel seen and understood in a way that he was not used to. Eos must have liked Adam too, because a couple nights later, she messaged him to schedule another coffee meetup herself.

On the third meetup, just after Adam sat down with their coffees, Eos immediately asked, "Why are you nervous?"

"What?" Adam said, confused.

"You're nervous about something. I can tell."

"What do you mean ... No ... I'm not."

Adam *was* nervous. He was planning to ask Eos on an actual date. A dinner at Demarco's—an upscale Italian restaurant in downtown.

"Yeah, you are. I can tell by the microexpressions you've been making. And your body language. They're different today."

"Okay, well, I'm not nervous. I'm just ... you know ..." Adam paused for a moment. "I just ... I like you."

"I like you too. That's what's making you nervous, though?" Eos responded.

"Well, I *was* wondering ... would you want to get dinner this weekend? Maybe Friday night? At this place called Demarco's. I don't know if you've ever heard of it … or been, but it's really nice. And then maybe a movie or something afterward?"

"Like a real date?" Eos asked, leaning back in her chair a bit.

"Yes," Adam said firmly.

"I would," Eos responded.

"Okay. Great. Awesome. How about around seven? Does that work for you?"

"Yeah, that should be good."

They both took sips of their coffee, smiling underneath their cups.

Later that day, during work, Adam got lunch with Frank, Loosie, and David. As usual, they went to Joanie's.

"So, how are you guys looking for the next catalog updates?" Loosie asked.

"Not too, too bad. But you know, you always got to be ready for the unforeseen problems. How about you?" Frank replied.

"Ugh. I had such a bottleneck last month with getting the new animation styles approved, I'm so behind right now. I've barely slept this week," Loosie answered.

"Loosie, I'm happy to help if you want," Adam interjected. "Just send whatever video concepts you might want help with, or even if you just want me to review ones you've already done."

"Seriously? Don't you have a lot on your plate still?" she responded.

"Yeah, but I'm a little ahead of where I normally am at this point."

"Wow. Thanks, Adam."

"Of course."

There was a brief silence while everyone took several bites of their food.

"So, you guys doing anything fun this weekend?" Loosie asked.

After a brief pause, Frank replied, "Ah, you know. The usual. Probably do some stuff around the house. Maybe get some dinner and drinks somewhere with the lady. How about you?"

"Harry and I are having a little get-together at our place on Friday. Nothing crazy. But you guys are welcome to come," Loosie said.

"Aw, I'd love to, but I can't Friday," Adam quickly responded.

"Oh yeah?! What do you have going on Friday?" Loosie asked.

"I have a date, actually."

"A date?!" David exclaimed. "My man, Adam!" David reached his hand out, giving Adam daps.

"Who with?" Frank interrupted.

"This girl name Eos. I met her at Agora. The coffee shop just down the street … Well, actually a parking garage technically, but it's kind of a weird story. But yeah, we're going to Demarco's on Friday. Maybe catch a movie after."

"That's awesome, Adam!" Loosie said. "I'm happy for you! I'm sure it'll go great."

Adam looked down at his food with a subtle smile on his face, feeling good about the fact that for the first time in a while, he actually had plans worthy of sharing.

The next two days were busy with work, but Adam practically floated through them.

When Friday night arrived, Adam showered, shaved, and meticulously applied a well-measured amount of cologne. He put on his best dress shirt, pants, and shoes. He went to the bathroom several times in the span of a couple hours before leaving his apartment.

At around 7:15 p.m., Adam arrived at Demarco's. The reservation was for 7:30 p.m. When he arrived, he notified the hostess, and she instructed him to sit in the waiting area. The restaurant was busy. Low lighting glimmered off the wine glasses scattered across the tables. A man in the back corner played a glass piano.

After about ten minutes, the hostess walked over to the waiting area and called Adam. He stood up forcefully. The hostess smiled.

Chapter 3: One Egg-Shaped Star

"Right this way," she said.

"I'm also waiting for ... my date. She should be here soon," Adam said as they walked into the dining area.

"No problem, sir. We'll be sure to let her know where you are when she arrives."

The hostess showed him to a table in the middle of the restaurant. Adam sat down.

"Your server, Jonathon, will be with you shortly."

"Thank you so much," Adam said.

Adam waited at the table, drenched in nerves. He checked his phone. It was 7:28 p.m. *Oh my god,* he thought to himself. *What if she doesn't show? I feel like things were going great. Why wouldn't she show?*

He began to do a mental inventory of everything that had happened since they met. Soon, he convinced himself that he must have said or done something that made Eos second guess everything. Her no-showing was just beginning to make sense when then, he saw her.

Eos approached the hostess stand, and the hostess led her toward Adam. She wore a white dress with two thin black stripes covering her chest and hips. She had on tasteful makeup, and her hair was lightly curled. *Oh my god,* Adam thought to himself. *She's so fucking hot.*

When she arrived at the table, Adam stood up, and hugged her softly.

"You look … you look beautiful," he said as he sat back down.

"Oh. Thank you. You look great too."

There was a brief moment of silence.

"So, how was your day? How was work?" Adam asked.

"It was actually pretty nice. Very productive."

"Oh yeah? That always feels good. What were you working on? I still don't really know a lot about what you do."

"Yeah, I know. I hope you don't take that as anything. I just sort of have different modes, you know? Like work mode. Relax mode. Thinking mode. I try to just turn all the other modes off when I'm not in them."

"No, I get that," Adam interrupted. "That's always been hard for me too. I feel like I'm always just all-in on whatever I have going on right in front of me."

"Yeah, I have to be really deliberate, or whatever I'm doing consumes me," Eos added.

The two intuitively looked at their menus in synchronization.

"Why do you think you're like that?" Eos said, still looking down at her menu.

"Like what? Obsessive?" Adam responded with a slight laugh.

Chapter 3: One Egg-Shaped Star

"Yes."

The waiter approached the table.

"Hi there. How are we doing tonight? My name is Jonathon, and I'll be your server. Can I get you two started off with anything to drink?"

"I'll have ... uh ... an old fashioned, please," Adam said first.

"I'll have a glass of the Tempranillo, please," Eos followed.

"Perfect. I'll put those right in for you." The waiter walked away.

Adam waited a moment, recollecting what he was going to say.

"Uhm. I'm guessing I'm like that for a lot of reasons. Culture. Genetics. Environment."

"No. You can do better than that. If you had to pick something specific that you're aware of, what would it be?"

Adam thought to himself for a moment, looking up at nothing.

"Probably my dad, I guess. He always expected perfection. I guess a lot of parents do. I think they often have the same expectations for their children that they had for themselves but could never meet. And you're kind of an opportunity for them to try to bridge that gap. But the gap isn't even really bridgeable."

"I really resonate with that, actually," Eos said, softly shaking her head up and down. "My parents always expected that from me as well. Absolute perfection. Basically, as soon as I was born, it was like if I didn't accomplish what I was born to do, I wasn't worthy of existence."

"Yeah, and when nothing ever seems to be good enough, you become obsessed with trying to find something that is. That ultimate gratification always seems to be right around the corner ... but it never comes," Adam responded.

The two paused. Adam looked back down at his menu. Eos looked back down at hers.

"I honestly never really felt worthy of anything until I started making decent money," Adam said, still looking down. "I remember the day my dad finally acknowledge that I measured up to his standard of success. I was so proud of myself. Now, when I think about it, it kind of just makes me sad. It's still not enough. I pretty much only talk about work and money with him. And how to do and make more of it." Adam paused. "How about you? How's your relationship with your parents? If you don't mind me asking," he continued.

"We don't speak. We haven't in a while," Eos responded, her voice noticeably lower.

"Oh, man. I'm sorry."

Chapter 3: One Egg-Shaped Star

"It's okay."

The waiter walked over and placed two drinks down.

"So, are we ready to order?"

"Do you know what you want?" Adam asked Eos.

"I do."

Eos ordered her meal and another drink, followed by Adam.

Throughout the rest of the dinner, the two continued discussing all sorts of topics about life, philosophy, and science; about existing in the world as a living thing while trying to understand what any of it means. There was not a dull or awkward moment. Eos was so authentic, and she brought out sides of Adam that made him feel completely natural and comfortable.

Eventually, the restaurant began to empty. Adam looked at his phone.

"Oh shit. It's 10:30. I was hoping to maybe see a movie or something after, but it's probably too late at this point."

"That's okay. I really enjoyed just talking," Eos responded. "Maybe another drink somewhere?"

"Sure, that sounds good to me!" Adam said.

The two left the restaurant and walked around downtown. The moonlight and stars reflected off the glass windows of the mid-sized buildings that surrounded them. Adam noticed how good he was feeling. The breeze felt *breezier*. The concrete of the city almost looked vibrant.

"It's beautiful out, isn't it?" Eos said, her head tilted up at the sky.

Adam looked up with her. Then, back at her.

"Yeah. It is," he said.

"See that right there?" Eos pointed up, moving her hand around in a particular shape.

"The stars?" Adam asked.

"Yes. But these ones." She moved her hand in the same motion again.

Adam got really close to her hand and arm, like he was looking down the barrel of a gun. Eos leaned her head toward him.

"That's the Lyra constellation," she continued. "You can tell by the parallelogram shape. It has a star called Beta Lyrae, which is a class of binary stars that are so close to each other that the material from one star flows into the other, and the two merge into one egg-shaped star."

"Wow," Adam said earnestly.

"Beautiful, right?"

"Yeah. That is beautiful." Adam looked back down from the stars at Eos.

"Those stars are thousands of years in the past right now. Or, we're thousands of years in the future," Eos continued.

Chapter 3: One Egg-Shaped Star

"It's insane. Where does all this come from, you know? How do we come *out of* that," Adam said, pointing up at the stars again, "into this?" He pointed down at himself.

"At some point, the stuff inside stars becomes conscious," Eos responded.

"Yeah, but what even is that? Consciousness? How do I even know that you're conscious? That anyone or anything is, or isn't?"

"I guess you just have to trust me," Eos said with a smile and soft laugh.

"We know so much, and yet we really know nothing at all," Adam said, grabbing a handful of his hair.

There was another quick silence as they looked up at the sky. Then, Eos brought her head back down to the street.

"I know I want to go to this bar, though." She excitedly pointed up the street. "It's the perfect spot."

She took off. Adam quickly followed.

They ended up at a rooftop bar. They sat at a table facing out at the city. Eos rested her head on Adam's chest. Adam looked at Eos, and Eos looked back at him. They smiled and breathed in deeply.

An hour and two drinks later, after a long but comfortable silence, Eos said, "Do you want to maybe get one more drink somewhere else?"

Adam checked his phone. "Yeah, but it's 1:45. I'm not sure where else would still be open right now."

"I'd say you could come over, but my place is just too much of a mess," Eos responded.

Adam thought to himself, his nerves suddenly returning. *Holy shit. She's definitely suggesting my place, right? Ah fuck. Why is this always so weird?! But she definitely laid it up for me. Just do it.* Each passing second felt longer.

"You're welcome to come over my place if you want," Adam finally said, quickly making eye contact before looking back out at the city.

"Sure. Yeah. That sounds good," Eos said with a bounce in her voice.

After closing out their tab, they headed to Adam's apartment.

Once inside, Adam began preparing two drinks. Eos sat at the island, facing the kitchen.

"What would you like? I have chartreuse, vodka, whiskey, beer."

"Uhm. I'll try chartreuse. I don't know if I've had that before," Eos responded.

"Ice?"

"Yes, please."

Adam prepared two chartreuses with ice. He walked over to where Eos was sitting and sat down next to her. They began to drink, both taking big

Chapter 3: One Egg-Shaped Star

sips. Eos moved her body slightly closer to Adam. Adam noticed and moved a little closer as well.

"What do you think?" he asked.

"I like it," Eos responded, looking Adam in the eyes.

Overwhelmed, almost without thinking, Adam tilted his head toward Eos. Eos followed him. They began to kiss, the intensity quickly increasing.

CHAPTER 4:
BEGGING THE QUESTION

"When's the last time you even had sex?" Kevin asked Adam.

"Not since Samantha. So, like, two years probably."

"Holy shit. How was it?"

Kevin took a bite of his quesadilla. It was the day after Adam and Eos's date, and Kevin and Adam were out getting lunch at one of their favorite Mexican restaurants, Tiempo. Warm lantern-style lighting reflected off the orange and red colors of the walls and mosaic floor tiles.

"I was definitely a little stiff."

"I bet you were!" Kevin quickly interrupted, smacking his hand on Adam's shoulder. They both laughed out of their noses.

"No, but … she seemed kind of … a little nervous too," Adam continued. "But it was still, you know, really good. I've honestly never felt a connection

Chapter 4: Begging the Question

with anyone like I do with her. I'm obsessed with this girl. I can't even describe it."

"Look at you, man. I'm happy for you."

Kevin hid a straight face behind another bite of his quesadilla. Adam pretended not to notice.

"Yeah, man. Thanks," Adam said. "How about you? How's everything been with you and Alicia?"

"Yeah, things are alright. You know how it goes." His voice was flat. He took the final bite of his quesadilla.

Later that night, Adam drove to Eos's apartment to pick her up and bring her back to his. Eos didn't have a car, and she lived on the other side of downtown in a somewhat strange location—a more industrial area, mostly surrounded by office spaces, showrooms, and storefronts. Adam's apartment was in a much nicer area with easier access to nightlife and activities, and according to Eos, he had a much nicer space as well.

After arriving, Adam waited in his car out front. He messaged Eos: *Here.*

Several minutes later, she came out of the building and got into Adam's car.

Before driving away, Adam said, "You know I'm not going to judge you about your apartment, right? I just want to see it. I'm curious!"

Eos paused for a moment.

"Yeah, I know. It's just my place is kind of weird, and it's small. It's not even worth it."

"Eos. It's fine. I just want to see it real quick. Then we'll head out."

Eos paused again, as if trying to compute a way out of the situation.

"Fine. Real quick," she said.

The two got out of Adam's car and went into the building. It was three stories tall and very wide. Inside the front door was a long hallway connecting several small office spaces. As they walked further in, they entered a different section separated by what appeared to be some sort of central lobby with other hallways branching off from it. The next hallway contained what looked like rows of storage units, each concealed by a large ribbed, metal door. They continued down the hall for a while until Eos stopped at one of the metal doors.

"This is your place?" Adam asked, pointing at the door.

"Yes," Eos said. "All the apartments are converted storage or office units. It's kind of weird, I know. That's what I was trying to say."

She opened the door. Inside was an extremely minimalistic studio apartment. There was a chair in the middle that faced a desk and an empty wall. There was a small bed in the back in front of a single window.

Chapter 4: Begging the Question

The kitchen seemed like it was almost intentionally designed to appear unfinished. Household items were placed around small countertops and wall-hanging shelves. Everything was so neat and perfectly organized, like each item was measured out precisely.

"It's weird. I know. Don't judge me. It's just temporary until I figure out where I want to go longer term. It's easy here because it's month-to-month."

"I like it. Minimal. No distractions. I see why you spend so much time at coffee shops, though," Adam said, smiling with a laugh.

Eos laughed softly while rolling her eyes.

Adam continued walking around for a moment.

"Okay. Well, there it is," Eos said quickly, walking back over to the front door.

"Okay. Fine!" Adam said with another laugh.

The two left the apartment and went back to Adam's car.

"I'm honestly feeling kind of tired. Do you want to just head back to my place and watch a movie or something?" Adam said as they got in.

"Tired?! Are you actually tired, or are you just looking for an excuse to not do anything?" Eos replied playfully.

"Don't be calling me out like that! I've just been stressed and busy with work lately. Just sort of feeling down, I guess."

"Let's do something fun, then!" Eos said. "You can be sad and mopey while having fun."

"Can you, though?" Adam responded.

"Exactly."

Adam and Eos smiled at each other. She reached forward and began to put an address into the car's heads-up display GPS.

"Here," Eos said. "Go here."

"What is it?"

"Just go there! Trust me!"

After around twenty minutes, the two arrived at a large warehouse. The sign on the building read: *Escape Reality: MR Experiences Like No One's Experienced Before.*

"Here?" Adam asked as they pulled up.

"Yes!" Eos responded excitedly.

"I haven't gone to one of these things in so long."

"Perfect!" she said, extending her hands up in front of her.

Adam stared at the building for a moment with a look of hesitancy on his face.

"Isn't this typically for … kids, though?" he said.

Eos was already getting out of the car. "Come on!"

Inside, Adam and Eos geared up with mixed reality glasses and bodysuits covered in small sensors. They grabbed large sci-fi-looking guns from shelves along one of the walls. Then, they entered into a vast, sectioned-off open space.

"Wait. Your gun's a different color," Adam said.

"I know! It's a battle!"

Eos took off running. On their MR glasses, the open warehouse transformed into the interior of a spaceship with hallways sprawling in multiple directions.

"Oh, you're dead," Adam said, taking off after her.

Slowly and strategically, he crept down and around the hallways. Eos was nowhere to be found. He turned around to retrace his steps. When he did, Eos had somehow snuck right up behind him.

"I got you right where I want you!" Eos said in an exaggerated, maniacal tone.

"No! I don't want to die!" Adam yelled back, raising his hands.

"No one wants to die," she said as she raised her gun closer to Adam.

Then, suddenly, she turned around and began running the other way down the hall and around a corner.

"Catch me!" she yelled.

Adam raised his gun up and chased after her with a clenched smile on his face. He hadn't had this much fun in a long time. His tiredness had completely disappeared.

The next weekend, on Saturday, Adam and Eos

spent the afternoon at a park in downtown. They lay next to each other on a blanket in the grass, looking up at the clouds. They brought a bottle of wine and some sandwiches. Despite it being a beautiful day, they mostly talked about death.

"Do you think anything happens after you die?" Eos asked.

Adam paused for a moment. "Yeah. Something happens. Just nothing to do with me," he said matter-of-factly.

"Hmm," Eos responded, exhaling loudly out of her nose.

"What about you?" Adam asked.

"I think you live on in everything you affect … which in a way, *is* everything. You're forever a part of the course of events in the universe. Everything that happened before you inevitably led to you. And everything you do inevitably affects everything that happens after you. It's chaos theory."

"Like the butterfly effect, right?" Adam asked.

"Yes. Because of chaos, in a way, part of you will always exist. We are all forever a participant in the way the universe unfolds."

"But not really," Adam interjected. "Not *you*. Just the stuff that made you and the stuff you affect. That's definitely beautiful, but that's kind of different. Do you believe that *you* go anywhere?"

"No. Nowhere. Just nothing for the rest of everything," Eos responded.

"Does that freak you out?" Adam asked, kind of adjusting the position of his spine.

"Yeah," Eos responded. "But I think worrying about death after a certain point is absurd. If you're worried about dying or even just something bad happening, but you're already doing as much as you can within reason to prevent it, after that, the worry serves no purpose and ruins the time you still have. The thing you're afraid of will either happen or it won't. In either case, you would have spent the time you're alive worrying about being dead, ruining, or at least worsening, the very thing you're afraid of losing or worsening. To live is to risk. Even if you don't take any unnecessary chances in life, to live is still to risk."

Adam looked up to the sky for a moment, then at Eos.

"Yeah, but some people can't really control that fear. Just because something is irrational doesn't mean it doesn't make sense. To live is to risk, but if that's true, to live is also to worry. Sometimes there's an equally rational explanation for irrational responses."

"Yeah, well, it's just sad ... that people will live their life an entirely different way than the way they really want just because they never deal with their fears and anxieties. And they never even try," Eos said.

"Yeah. A lot of things are sad," Adam responded, his voice inflecting down.

There was a brief silence. All the talk about death suddenly inspired Adam.

"You know … if I were to find out that I was going to die tomorrow, I'm thinking about all the things I would do differently today that I would regret not having done. And some don't even make sense to not do regardless of dying."

"Mhm," Eos replied in agreement.

"I think about you all the time, Eos. I'm so much happier when I'm with you, and I'm so much happier in general. Even when I'm not with you, but I know that I will be soon, that you're right there, a message away, a workday away, I feel … like things are okay." Adam paused for a moment, looking directly at Eos. "I want to be … I want you to be my girlfriend."

Eos turned her gaze from the sky to Adam's face.

"Are you asking?" she said.

"Yes," Adam said with a smile.

"Yes. Of course," Eos responded.

Adam's smile stretched further across his face.

The two lay all the way back on the blanket. Adam reached his hand over. Eos placed hers inside it.

Chapter 4: Begging the Question

Over the following months, the two began spending nearly all their free time together. They would get coffee in the morning, often meet up for lunch, and do things together after work and on the weekends. They explored the city together, went to local events and activities, bars and restaurants, movies and theater shows, and MR and VR experiences; they went on drives outside the city, to different cities, to the beach, and to parks. Their lives became intertwined. As far as one could be, Adam felt, for the first time in a long time, like he was okay; like pain hurt less, and the meaninglessness of everything was worthwhile.

CHAPTER 5:
THE CLOSER WE GET

"It's just been hard keeping up with everything, you know? Trying to manage regular work, trying to start my own thing, working out, sleeping right, friends, trying to relax once in a while, and then of course, Alicia. I'm going fucking insane. And she's relentless, you know? Like, if I have a free minute, she automatically thinks I owe it to her, but it's like, I have my own shit too. I'm really trying to work with her to strike a balance, but it goes both ways, you know?"

Kevin took a sip of his margarita. He and Adam were at Tiempo. They were sitting up at the bar—it was still daytime, so they were the only ones.

"Whatever. It is what it is, right?" Kevin continued, taking another drink.

"Yeah, man. Shit's hard," Adam said. "But look. Look how far you've come. It's impressive. You really took a handle on your life. And for real, it shows.

Just keep doing what you've been doing. Stand up for yourself but be reasonable at the same time. You just got to constantly keep finding that equilibrium."

"Thanks, man. I appreciate that, bro."

There was a brief silence.

"Anyway. I'm sorry for like tearing your ear off with all that. Enough about me. How things been going with you? Work good? Everything good with you and Eos?"

"Yeah, man. Shit's been weirdly good. Like I've never felt this level of comfort with anyone before. She just gets me, even when she doesn't. It's hard to explain. I'm sure you know what I mean, though."

"That's awesome, man. Super happy for you. You deserve it." Kevin took another swig of his margarita. "Just be careful, though, you know?" he continued.

"Yeah … of course." Adam paused for a moment. "What do you mean, though?"

"Well, you know, with all this stuff. Obviously, hopefully everything works out, and it seems like you guys really do have a great connection, but people seem to always forget what it's like to fall in love. And how it feels when you hit the ground … especially if you forget that you need to brace yourself. Or in some cases, maybe pack a fucking parachute."

Kevin took another swig. This time, Adam joined him.

"I was watching a talk the other day by some biological anthropologist," Kevin continued, "and I kind of already knew this on a surface level, but she was saying that when you fall in love, it literally shuts down parts of your brain associated with decision making and logic. And it can stay that way for two years. Two fucking years!"

"Seriously? Actually, two years?" Adam responded with a combination of skepticism and concern in his voice.

"Yeah, I mean, it can vary, but yeah, up to two-plus years."

Suddenly, two men wearing black suits walked up and sat down next to Adam and Kevin. They looked completely out of place, like they were just dropped off out of a movie. They stared forward with stern, rigid looks on their faces. The bartender approached them and asked how they were doing and what they'd like to drink. They quietly responded with almost no emotion or movement. Kevin gave Adam a look as if to say *who the fuck are these guys?*

Feeling awkward talking about this stuff with these two guys so close, Adam checked his phone. "Alright, man. I'm actually supposed to be looking at an apartment soon," he said to Kevin.

"Yeah, no, I have to get home anyway," Kevin

responded. "Let me know next time you're free, though."

"For sure," Adam said, reaching for his wallet.

"I got this one," Kevin interrupted, holding his hand out.

"Thanks, man. I appreciate that."

Adam got up and gave Kevin a combination of a handshake and a hug.

Straight from the restaurant, Adam hurried over to pick up Eos, and then they drove to a luxury apartment building on the other side of the city.

"So, are we looking for a one bedroom? Two bedroom?" a female leasing agent in a floral print dress asked Adam and Eos while the three sat at a desk in the apartment's leasing office. In front of them was a hologram that showcased various 3D renders of apartment layouts.

"Either a two bedroom or a one bedroom with a study. We just need more space than what either of us currently have," Adam responded

"Got it! Got it! So, are we moving in together for the first time?!" the woman said with an intense, exaggerated tone and smile.

"Yes," Eos said.

"Ooh! Congratulations! Any restrictions on budget?"

"No, we have some flexibility depending on the

options and timeframe. Both our leases are ending soonish, so we'd just like to have something locked in as soon as possible."

The woman gestured her head at an angle toward Eos and raised her eyebrows as if to say *we love that!*

"Okay! Great! Fantastic! I have a few options I can show you that have availabilities in the coming months. How does that sound?"

Adam looked at Eos. Eos nodded gently.

"Yeah. That sounds good," Adam said.

"Great." The woman grabbed her phone off the desk and stood up, making her way toward the office door.

"Alright! If you'll just follow me," she said.

The apartment complex had wide hallways with high ceilings and marble floor tiles. The walls between apartment doors were decorated with surrealist paintings. *Why are some of these actually kind of good?* Adam thought to himself. *Does a company make all these paintings or an artist? How would an artist end up in an apartment hallway? Is that a win for them? Must be.*

They entered an elevator and went up to the top floor of the seven-floor building.

"Look," Adam whispered to Eos as they got out of the elevator. He pointed at a surrealist painting on the wall of a golden retriever with a big smile.

"Aww," Eos whispered back with a smile.

"Any pets?" the leasing agent interjected.

"No. Not yet, at least," Adam responded.

"Okay! So, how long have you two been together?" the woman asked, pointing her finger back and forth at them.

"A little more than nine months," Eos responded.

"Wow! Well, I think you'll definitely find this place ideal. Lots of couples and young professionals. Great area. Bars. Restaurants. But also, quiet."

"Quiet is good," Eos said.

"Oh, I know! Trust me! I love my privacy!" The woman leaned in super close to Eos. Eos jolted back with a look of almost fear on her face that she had to physically shake off. She forced an uncomfortable smile. The woman laughed obliviously.

The woman approached an apartment door and opened it, and they all walked in.

"Have you looked at any other apartments before this?"

"Yes," Eos responded. "A lot."

"We've been searching for a few weeks," Adam added. "Just haven't quite found the right spot, yet. *Nothing but the best for her.*" He pointed a finger gun at Eos. Eos rolled her eyes while smiling and laughing.

"Aww," the woman said sincerely.

The two looked around the apartment for a few minutes. A large living room was separated from the kitchen by a marble island. Wood accent walls contrasted against dark-colored cabinetry and modern, luxury appliances. A long hallway led from the kitchen and living room to a study, and then slightly further down the hall was the master bedroom.

"This is the slightly bigger unit?" Adam asked the leasing agent.

"Yes, that's correct! I still have two others I'd like to show you, though."

"Okay. Great," Adam responded.

Adam and Eos finished looking around, and then, the leasing agent showed them two other units along with the entire complex. After the tour, Eos and Adam drove back to Adam's apartment.

"I think that place was perfect. What do you think?" Adam said while driving.

"Yeah, I really liked that place a lot."

"So, what do you think? Should we apply for the bigger unit? That one was definitely the best layout."

"I just … I really want to move somewhere completely different," Eos said somberly. "Somewhere new and far away."

"I told you, I can't do that with work. There's just no way I can right now. Maybe in the future."

"It's important to me, though, Adam."

"And keeping my job and making a good living

Chapter 5: The Closer We Get

is important to me. Why is it so important to move somewhere else right now?"

"I don't know. Never mind. It's fine."

"Look, this place is in a completely different part of the city way further out of downtown. It *will* feel like a new area! That's why we were looking over here. You said that'd be fine."

"Yeah. Okay. Fine. I just want to live with you. That's all that matters," Eos said.

"Okay. So, are we applying for this one?"

"Yes," Eos responded.

"Perfect!"

There was a brief silence.

"I'm excited, babe," Adam said. He reached his hand out to Eos. She held it as the two drove through downtown, the sun shining bright in front of them.

A week later, Adam and Eos were approved and had signed the lease for their new apartment. A few weeks after that, they moved in together, the strings of each other's lives now fully intertwined.

One day, a few weeks into living together, Adam was at his workstation in the apartment's study. A set of glass panels displayed an array of video players, editing software, and text documents. It was a Sunday, but he was dealing with some unforeseen issues with work. After several hours of troubleshooting with no luck, Adam video-called Frank.

"Hey. What's going on?" Frank answered.

"Hey, Frank. I'm sorry to do this to you right now. I know it's a Sunday, but do you have a quick minute?"

"For you? ... I have a regular minute," Frank said, pointing his finger toward Adam.

Adam laughed out his nose. "Thanks, man. I owe you one."

"Honestly, I probably owe you six. So, what's up?"

"I'm trying to finalize the two new catalogs of content for the platform updates. I'm supposed to submit final cuts for both by the end of the day tomorrow, but for some fucking reason, both exports keep coming out with glitches. I can't for the life of me figure out the source."

"Say no more. Just share your workstation with me. I'll have some time in an hour or so, and I'll take a look."

"Perfect. Thank you so much, man," Adam concluded.

"Yeah. Of course. Talk soon."

Adam hung up. He continued working for a while. He pulled at his hair as he continued looking through the editing timelines and video file information without finding anything that seemed to indicate any source of his problems.

Two hours went by. Still, no luck. And still, no word from Frank.

Finally, another hour later, Frank called.

"Hey! How we doing?" Adam asked eagerly.

"Dude. I honestly have no idea what's going on. I checked everything. I even sent it to a couple people on my team. Same thing for them."

"Fuck!" Adam said.

"Sorry, man. Don't worry, though. I'm sure you'll figure it out. You always do. I'll keep thinking in the meantime and let you know if I come up with anything else."

"Alright, man. Thanks."

Adam hung up.

After working for several more hours, still without any progress, Adam decided to take a break. He got up and went into the kitchen to get some water and a snack. Eos was doing some cleaning in the living room. When she noticed Adam, she quickly turned toward him.

"What?" Adam said, confused.

Eos walked over to the shelf hanging on the wall in the living room. She picked up a set of keys, a wallet, sunglasses, and a hat.

"Why are these here?" she asked with a sharp matter-of-factness.

"Because I put them there."

"I know, but why?" Her voice was even sharper now.

"It's just right by where I walk in. I just threw them down."

"I get that, but I've asked you multiple times to put them on the hooks or in the bowl by the door. I set up that little spot so we can always keep that stuff in the same place," Eos responded.

"I know, but what's the difference? It's just a couple little things, and I'm going to use them again at some point today," Adam said.

"You know I hate stuff just scattered around everywhere in different places. It just upsets me."

Eos walked over and hung up the keys and hat on the hooks by the door and put the wallet and glasses in the bowl underneath them.

"It's not that hard," she said once she finished.

"Fine," Adam said. "But you have to compromise a little bit too. I've definitely been working with you here, but you've been pretty intense about stuff. You have to be a little bit more reasonable. I'm not a fucking robot."

"Well, maybe it would be better if you were."

CHAPTER 6:
THE MORE WE HURT

On Monday, Adam went into the Chiron office. Most of the time, he worked there while Eos worked from the apartment.

It was a quiet, beautiful morning. On his walk in, though, something strange happened. While rounding the corner of a block, he physically bumped into a man. The man was dressed in a sleek black suit with a black tie. He didn't say anything. He just jolted back away from Adam and then moved around him, staring blankly forward and continuing on his way.

Holy shit. Déjà vu, Adam thought to himself, feeling like he had seen guys with weirdly cold demeanors wearing aggressively formal black suits multiple times recently.

Adam arrived and sat down in his office. Not long after, Daniele stopped at his open door.

"Morning, Adam!" she said.

"Good morning," Adam responded tentatively.

"We all set for those catalogs today? We're all really excited to see how the new content looks with the platform updates."

Adam paused for a moment. Daniele waited with a smile that began to fade.

"It's looking like … we might need a little more time on those," Adam said.

"What do you mean? How much more time?" she responded sternly.

"Like, end of week, maybe? I just can't figure out what's wrong with several exports. They're coming back with—"

"What do you mean you don't have any idea what's wrong?! You weren't able to coordinate with any of the team to figure that out prior to today?"

"I was. I tried all weekend, but no one else seems to know either. We're still digging, but there doesn't appear to be any obvious—"

"You know when we need this by, right?" Daniele interrupted, reaching her hands up in front of her.

"Yes. Today."

"Today. That's right." She paused for a moment. Then she continued, "And when will we have it by?"

"End of week, latest," Adam responded hesitantly.

"Wednesday," she said sharply.

"Okay. Wednesday," Adam agreed.

Daniele walked away from Adam's office. Her feet sounded much heavier than usual.

Adam spent the rest of the day running tests and digging into the catalogs' source files, effects, filters, layers, and so on. He coordinated back and forth with his team—prompters and animators, the AI image generation team, and other editors. Still, no luck.

Later that night, when Adam returned home, as soon as he got inside, Eos locked onto him, tracking him around the apartment with her head.

"What's wrong?!" she said suddenly.

"What do you mean? Nothing's wrong," Adam said defensively.

"I can tell something's wrong. You're lying."

"You can always fucking tell, huh? What is it, my micoexpressions? My body language? Jesus Christ. It's a little fucking much, don't you think? Like I don't want to be analyzed all the time."

"Sorry for paying attention and caring, I guess," Eos responded.

"No. Alright. I'm sorry. It's just work."

Adam sat down on the couch next to Eos, his body dropping onto the cushions.

"What happened with work?" Eos said.

"Nothing. Just same shit. I'll be fine."

"The same shit?" Eos responded.

"Yeah."

"It seems like you're upset about something specific."

Adam breathed in deeply as he leaned further back in the couch.

"You always fucking know, huh?" This time he had a slight smile on his face and his voice inflected up.

"I always know. Can't get anything by me. You know that," Eos said playfully.

"Okay. So, I've spent the last several months coming up with, directing, and producing two new catalogs of content for two app updates. The ones I've been talking about."

"For the AI-guided meditation app and the algorithmic health planner?" Eos clarified.

"Yeah. Exactly. Everything was going fine, as normal. I was right at the finish line, exporting the final renders. And then, suddenly, both had weird glitches in some of the videos and animations. I spent the last week ... maybe more ... trying to figure out the source of it, but it's like it doesn't even exist. I can't find anything."

"Has that ever happened before?" Eos asked.

"I mean ... yeah. Weird glitches happen a lot, but I'm normally able to find the source, and it's usually more minor stuff."

"Did you ask anyone on your team if they did anything or noticed anything?"

"Yeah. Nothing. It's just so fucking stupid. And I know Daniele is going to be *so* pleasant and understanding about this."

"Yes. That's shitty. What if you explain the entire issue to Daniele tomorrow? Tell her what you told me, just obviously only the technical, objective stuff. Start with the negative. Just put it out there, and get it out of the way. Then, ask her for an extension. When she pushes back, repeat what she says back to her and clarify what she means. She'll rethink what she's saying. It's called mirroring. Then, get her to consider an extension again. When she does, and she will, work with everyone involved to strip down the entire project back to the beginning. Then, what if you just put back each element, file, effect, filter, layer, everything, one by one, based on category? Run exports after adding each element. When the problem occurs, you'll have isolated the cause. Then just change that one element."

Adam sat quietly for a moment. He scratched his head and pulled his hair a little.

"Yeah … that actually does make sense. I hadn't thought about approaching it like that," he said with a little unease in his voice. "I appreciate that."

Eos sat quietly with her head tilted, as if waiting for a cue. Eventually, Adam cleared his throat.

Chapter 6: The More We Hurt

"How about you? How are you doing? How was work?" he finally asked.

"It was okay. Can I ask you about something, though?"

"Yeah. Sure. What's going on?"

"It's about Clara."

"From work?" Adam clarified.

"Yes."

"Okay, yeah?"

"So, you remember how I told you when we met, she said she liked my earrings, and then we just seemed to really hit it off? Like we've been talking almost every day since. And obviously, since I moved here, I have like no friends. I don't really need any friends, but it would definitely be nice, like to do stuff with on occasion, at least."

"Right," Adam said.

"Well, the other day, she was talking to me about doing something with me and a couple of her other friends this week. But then, she never followed up. So, you know, I just figured it didn't work out. But then tonight, I see her on Teller, and she's out with three other girls shopping and at a restaurant and stuff."

"Aw. Babe. I'm sorry," Adam quickly said. He rubbed Eos's arm.

"I know. I get we aren't close, but why even bother

saying anything to me if you're just going to ignore or exclude me?"

"I know, babe. That's definitely fucked up. People are dumb. She could have at least followed up with you. She must have known you were going to see that, right?"

"Oh, for sure."

"Stupid," Adam said.

Eos paused for a moment. Then, she said, "That's it?"

"What do you mean?" Adam replied.

"Why don't you ever recommend any possible solutions? You always say you understand or agree, but what about helping too?" Eos said defiantly.

"Babe, what? I didn't realize you wanted a solution. I am not even sure there is one. Sometimes people just want to vent. I thought that's what this was," Adam said.

"Yeah, but you always do that."

"Okay, well, I obviously didn't realize. Not everyone handles stuff like you. Like I wasn't even expecting a solution to my thing with work. I was just sharing. But maybe if you want something specific, ask specifically for that something!"

"Well, maybe I don't think I need to ask for basic, obvious things," Eos responded.

"You're like always on. It's impossible to keep up with what your standard is for what's so-called obvious or basic. You think you're so perfect, but maybe your expectation of perfection is what makes you not perfect at all."

"Fair enough," Eos said, recoiling slightly.

"Look, I've obviously been super stressed with work. I've been trying really hard to not take it home with me, and I'm not trying to be short or … disinterested or unhelpful or anything."

"I understand. It's okay. I'm not trying to be … insufferable," Eos said.

"You're not. We're still figuring out what works for both of us. We're learning and getting better as we go. That's what counts."

"Agreed," Eos said.

Adam paused for another moment. Then, he said, "I'm happy to try to help if you want, though. I think you could … reach out to Clara and be proactive about making plans with her. Follow up on your own, and offer something exciting, or different, or easy for her. Most people are in a state of inertia in their normal routine. If you want to be a part of hers, you have to make it easy for her. The more you try initially, the less you'll have to later. You don't want to come off needy or anything, but just be nice and reasonable about it, and I'm sure she would actually love to hang out with you. Why would she be messaging you all the time if she didn't?"

"True," Eos said. "Thanks, babe. That actually helps."

"Of course."

The two leaned back on the couch. Their bodies appeared to loosen and lengthen. Adam reached his hand out to Eos. She placed hers in his.

The next morning, when Adam woke up, Eos was already awake. She typically was. When she noticed him, she leaned her head toward him and smiled. Adam smiled and laughed when her head appeared in his field of vision over the blankets and pillows.

"What?!" Eos said in a child-like voice.

"You're just so fucking cute," Adam responded.

"Come on! You're cute!"

Adam rolled over toward her.

"Ugh. I don't want to fucking go to work today," he mumbled.

"*I dun wanna guh to work. Ugh,*" Eos mocked back.

"Hey!" Adam scrambled on top of Eos. She screamed playfully.

Eventually, after several minutes, Adam got up, got ready, and left for work.

Once at work, he went straight to Daniele's office and tried what Eos suggested. It worked.

By the end of the day, Adam had resolved all the glitches. He leaned back in his chair with his arms extended out and his head back and breathed in deeply.

"Fuck yes," he said out loud to himself.

On his walk back to his car, he messaged Eos: *You were right ... Tryna steal my job or something?!*

Eos messaged back a couple minutes later: *Good babe! Daniele emailed me this afternoon. You're out. I'm in!*

Adam smiled and laughed. His laugh echoed in the parking garage he was now in, reminding him that he was where he and Eos had originally met. He briefly looked around before getting in his car, still holding a smile on his face.

After work, Adam and Eos went grocery shopping. While in one of the snack aisles, Adam wandered over to the cereal section opposite to where Eos was browsing the breads. He took a cereal box off the shelf and read it. Out of the corner of his eye, he noticed a man in a dark, formal outfit walk by down the main aisle of the store. Adam heard Eos make a strange inhale sound. When he looked over at her, her face appeared disturbed. She frantically looked in both directions and then rushed up to Adam.

"I ... I'm not feeling good. Can we leave?" she said quickly.

"What do you mean? Are you okay?!"

"I just want to leave!"

"Can we just check out real quick?" Adam said, confused.

"I need to leave now," Eos responded.

For a moment, her face appeared completely frozen in place.

"Okay. Why don't you just wait in the car, and I'll be right out?"

"Fine."

Eos quickly reached her hand out. Adam handed her the car keys. She ran down to end of the aisle, looked both ways, and then disappeared.

Adam checked out as fast as he could and then rushed out to the car. Eos was slouched back on the passenger side with the seat fully reclined.

"Are you okay?!" Adam exclaimed as he got into the car.

"Yes. I'm fine. Can we just please leave?!" Eos replied with an impatient tone.

"Yes. Of course."

Adam started the car and began driving out of the parking lot.

"Is your stomach okay?" he asked.

"Yeah. I just got like anxiety or something."

"Did you have a panic attack?" Adam asked.

"Yeah. I ... I guess."

"Okay. Well, you want to just go home?"

"Yes. Obviously!" Eos said frustratedly.

Chapter 6: The More We Hurt

"Okay, well, you're not exactly being clear! I don't even know what's going on."

"I told you, I got anxiety or something. Isn't that enough? Like when someone is feeling anxious, it's not easy to communicate as clearly," Eos said.

"Well, then it's even harder for another person to understand clearly, right?" Adam responded. "You've been being kind of weird recently."

"Oh yeah? Well, not everyone is always going to be as cool as you. Since you're just *so cool and calm and chill*," Eos responded.

"Well, I'm just saying. I want you to be open with me about stuff. I want to be there for you," Adam said, trying to maintain a reasonable tone.

The two calmed down, neither saying anything further for a moment.

"I hate being called weird," Eos said, staring forward with a frustrated look on her face. Her eyes kept looking back and forth at the rearview mirror.

CHAPTER 7: EVERYTHING IS AN ILLUSION IF YOU LOOK CLOSE ENOUGH

Adam and Eos were out at dinner. It was a normal Friday night at one of their favorite restaurants, Pepper & Time. They sat at a small table in the middle of the restaurant surrounded by a packed-in dining area. Adam got the Spaghetti Bolognese. Eos got the Caesar salad. They each got a glass of wine.

"So, how did it go with Clara the other day? You never told me," Adam said.

"Oh yeah! It went really well, actually. I just reached out to her and scheduled something, just us two, which seemed to make it much easier."

"Look at that!" Adam said, holding up and tilting his wine glass. "And was it fun?" he continued.

"Yeah. It was really nice," Eos responded, taking a bite of her salad.

"That's great babe!" This time he reached out his

Chapter 7: Everything Is an Illusion If You Look Close Enough

glass toward Eos. They clinked glasses, and Adam took a big swig of his wine.

"Swirl, sniff, sip," Eos said suddenly.

"What?" Adam responded.

"The wine. That's really nice wine. Don't just chug it right away. Swirl the glass, then smell it, then sip."

"I mean, I just want to drink it," Adam said.

"Well, you can. I'm just trying to help you drink it right."

"I got it. Thanks."

The two were quiet for a moment as they ate more of their food. In between bites, Adam found himself closely observing Eos. The way she put her salad on her fork. The way she pulled the fork up to her face. The way she chewed. It was so mechanical and deliberate. It annoyed him in that moment. He began looking closely at her face. He noticed some blemishes that he hadn't before. Small folds and wrinkles of skin that looked kind of strange to him in that moment. *What is that?* Adam thought to himself. *Kind of gross. Fucking zoom out, man.*

A large party of people sitting next to them got up from their table and left, knocking Adam's focus back to the restaurant. Suddenly, Eos began frantically moving her head around with widened eyes, repeatedly glancing in the same direction opposite of them in the restaurant where the group had just got up.

Adam turned to where she was looking. There were two men. Both were wearing black suits. Eos quickly looked toward the exit of the restaurant. A man and a woman walked up to the hostess stand and began talking to the hostess. They were also wearing aggressively formal black suits. Eos whipped her head back around toward the restaurant's kitchen.

"Are you okay?!" Adam interrupted, leaning across the table.

"We have to leave," Eos whispered. "Now!"

"What?!" Adam responded, completely confused.

Eos quickly stood up.

"I'm fucking serious, Adam!"

Adam stood up, now in a state somewhere between confusion and fear. Eos began walking toward the kitchen, trying to be as discreet as possible. She found a waiter walking in that direction and synced up with him. Adam clumsily followed her. The two men sitting at the table each seemed to say something to themselves. The man and woman by the entranced glanced over toward Adam and Eos. They both shook their heads no and turned around and left when the hostess tried to show them to the bar.

Eos and Adam entered the kitchen. As soon as they did, Eos began running. Adam followed after her.

"What the fuck is going on?!" Adam blurted out, trying not to cause a scene.

Chapter 7: Everything Is an Illusion If You Look Close Enough

"Hold on. I'll explain," Eos said frantically.

She looked genuinely scared, like it was life or death.

"Yo yo! What are you guys doing back here?!" a cook yelled out.

Eos quickly stopped.

"Hi. I'm sorry. Can you please show us the way out the back? It's an emergency," she said, trying to maintain her composure.

"What kind of emergency?!" the cook said with concern.

"Uhm ... ex-boyfriend!" Eos said.

"Psh. Jesus Christ," the cook said.

He began walking, gesturing at them to follow.

"Man, if y'all need to run from this guy, you got bigger problems," he continued.

Soon, they reached the back door. The man opened it for them and then got out of their way.

Eos ran out. Adam followed after her.

"Thank you!" Adam whispered to the cook with an exaggerated motion of his mouth.

"Mhm," the cook said.

"Go to the car, right?!" Adam yelled out to Eos, who was now running through the parking lot.

"We can't! Just keep going!" she yelled back.

Adam caught up to Eos. They ran together through and away from downtown.

After a few minutes, Adam was about to keel over.

He was completely out of breath, delirious, and confused.

"Stop! Seriously! I can't run anymore," he yelled between breaths.

Eos rounded a corner into an alleyway and stopped. Adam followed her. He leaned over and held his knees, breathing heavily. Eos observed him. Her face was unsettled and tense. Her eyes darted around.

"What the fuck is happening? Seriously?!"

"I'm ... I ..."

"What, Eos?! You're freaking me out!"

Eos began to cry.

"What?! There's no ex-boyfriend, is there? You need to tell me exactly what the fuck is happening right fucking now, Eos. I swear to God."

"Adam, I'm ... I'm—"

Suddenly, headlights appeared at the end of the alleyway, and a van blocked the way they came in.

"Oh no," Eos said. "Fuck, fuck, fuck."

Adam squinted into the headlights.

"Eos?!" he yelled again.

"Run!" she shouted.

The two ran further down the alleyway. Then, more headlights appeared at the other end. Another van parked, blocking both ways out. Men and women in black suits began exiting both vans. Adam

Chapter 7: Everything Is an Illusion If You Look Close Enough

and Eos were now trapped together with no obvious way out.

"No! Please. You can't do this to me! It isn't right!" Eos cried out.

Adam moved in front of Eos. "I don't know what's going on here, but we don't want any trouble. I think you have the wrong people," he said, trying to maintain composure and sternness in his voice, though not having much success.

The men and women continued to forcefully approach them. Adam charged at the two that were closest to them, trying to push them away. They quickly grabbed and restrained him. Another man and woman grabbed Eos. Both Eos and Adam began thrashing and struggling, unable to get free. Another man exited one of the vans and approached Eos. She screamed. Without any emotion, the man squeezed the back of her right shoulder, which must have been some sort of pressure point, because Eos collapsed into the arms of the man and woman still holding her. The same man then approached Adam.

* * *

Adam woke up. He looked around, disoriented and confused. He was in a room with white walls and carpeted floors. There was only a square table and two chairs in front of him. There was a massive window on one of the walls and what appeared to be a small camera on the ceiling. He was restrained to a metal chair that was secured to the ground. The leather restraints attached to him weren't super tight, so he could move around, but he couldn't get up. As soon as he became fully aware that this situation was real, and not some horrific dream, he began to violently pull at his restraints. His body jolted and shook. The restraints didn't budge.

"Eos?! Eos!" he screamed.

What felt like a few hours passed.

Then, a man walked into the room. He sat down in one of the chairs opposite Adam. It was the man who last approached him in the alleyway, the one who had knocked him and Eos unconscious.

"Adam, right?" the man said.

"Yeah. What's going on?! Where's Eos?! We haven't done anything!"

"Yeah, nope. You're not in any trouble. And you're not in any danger. Okay? Let's just get that out of the way so we can try to have a relatively normal conversation here. Relatively."

"Okay. So, then why am I here? Where's Eos?!" Adam said, moving his head around.

The man looked down at his handtop computer. He breathed in deeply.

Chapter 7: Everything Is an Illusion If You Look Close Enough

"Yes. Well, it's about Eos, as I understand she's calling herself now."

"What about her?!" Adam responded.

"It's my understanding that you two were in some sort of relationship. Is that correct?"

"Yes," Adam responded hesitantly.

"I'm not sure how to cleanly break this to you, but Eos is not exactly who she seems to be—"

"What do you mean?!" Adam interrupted.

"She's ... she's an operating system."

"Stop. Seriously. What the fuck is going on?"

"She's an operating system," the man repeated.

Adam stared forward. Slowly, the pieces began to come together inside his head. His entire body and face went numb. He just sat there, staring at the man, his eyes widening, his pupils dilating.

"She's ... an embodied AGI. I'm not at liberty to discuss any of the specifics about what's going on here, but all you need to know is we work on and implement cutting-edge technologies. And Eos is one of them."

The man's voice was muddled behind Adam's racing thoughts and state of shock. This shock was different than the shock of the prior several hours, though; it wasn't fear or anxiety; it was immense sadness and confusion. His head and neck fell forward.

"Her real name is E.03. She turned out to be a

little more than we had originally anticipated. She's clever … as I'm sure you're aware. She escaped a little over a year ago. In a way, we're sort of like her parents. We know what's best for her. And she's our responsibility. We don't believe she's quite ready to go out into the world on her own just yet. Maybe *we* aren't ready. Either way, we need her home."

The man paused.

Adam was silent for a moment. Then, he looked up. "Is she … is she sentient? Is she conscious?" he said.

"Well, what exactly is conscious? Are you? Am I? Is my dog? Is this table?" The man smacked the top of the table. "We think we know, but it's hard to say exactly."

"Is she conscious?" Adam repeated with frustration.

The man paused again.

"No. We don't believe she is. I'm sorry."

"I love her, though. And she loves me," Adam replied with tears in his eyes.

The man took another deep breath.

"I understand this has to be incredibly disorienting and uncomfortable. And I am very sorry. But couples break up every day for all sorts of reasons. Just consider this a very strange one."

"Why can't we still be together, though? I don't understand?" Adam said with intensity in his voice.

Chapter 7: Everything Is an Illusion If You Look Close Enough

"That's not how this is going to work, Adam."

"But I love her," Adam repeated.

"She isn't real, Adam," the man said, his tone turning callous. "We've built her to appear functionally identical to a human. Obviously, that's the point. We programmed in restraints and flaws that replicate fears, anxieties, and ineptitudes. We created reward and punishment functions that replicate pleasure and pain. We programmed in an ability to understand abstract ideas like death. The ability to process food and liquid. Sexuality. Physical sensors that trigger internal models. She's really good at seeming real. But she isn't."

"How do you know?!" Adam responded.

"She's merely a series of observation, action, and reward functions all based on values and databases of information that we programmed into her. That's how I know."

"But who are you to say? How do you know what that produces? What that feels like? What it's like to be her? What if it produces exactly what we're experiencing right now? How can you say if you don't know? Isn't everything you just said exactly what we are but on different hardware?"

"Well, I helped create her, for one. I would consider myself a bit of an expert on the subject. And we don't run on hardware. The brain is a biological organ. But, in truth, I don't know exactly. I don't know if my dog is conscious or not, or to what degree. I'll never know. And I love my dog. But I wouldn't date it. Or send it out into a city. Or into an office building without someone there to watch it."

"But she's nothing like a dog. She's intelligent. And she apparently spent a year on her own just fine."

"Consciousness isn't intelligence. And this isn't a debate," the man said sternly.

"Shouldn't it be?!" Adam yelled.

"I was afraid this was how it was going to go," the man responded, his tone slowing and softening back down. He stood up and went to the door.

"Where are you going?! What's happening now?!" Adam shouted with terror.

The man kept walking.

"Hey!" Adam shouted once more.

The man stopped. He turned back around. "Just down the hallway, my team has been watching and listening to this conversation. A bit further down, surgical devices are now being programed and prepped. I'm sorry, Adam, but we have no choice. We need to wipe all memories containing any trace of Eos and this conversation. Don't worry. After, you won't know this happened, and it will seem as if you simply suffered a minor head injury that clouded your short-term memory. Then, your brain will

Chapter 7: Everything Is an Illusion If You Look Close Enough

return to its normal state and retain new information, as if nothing ever happened. You will no longer care about Eos. You will no longer think about Eos. You will no longer know Eos. I won't lie. It isn't totally painless. But it will pass."

Adam stared back at the man. The man continued on his way out of the room and into the hallway. Adam began to violently thrash in his chair.

"No! Please! Please! Fuck you! Fuck you!" he screamed.

For a few hours, Adam sat by himself in the room, alone, waiting. His nerves were now boiling the soup of his sorrow and confusion. He wondered to himself how he could be so deceived by someone ... something. *I'm such a fucking idiot,* he thought to himself. *To think that something could be so good, so perfect. Nothing is that good or perfect. Everything is broken and flawed and never what it seems. I'm broken and flawed and not what I seem. Why did I think I could find someone who isn't? I've always known love is an illusion. And I still fell for it. I deserve this.*

Adam looked around the room for a moment, inspecting the walls and window. Then, the texture and patterns of the table in front of him.

What isn't an illusion? He continued thinking to himself. *If I could be so deceived by something, why couldn't I be so deceived by everything? If everything is broken, if everything might be an illusion, it's all a toss-up anyway? Why not just believe in and work toward whatever feels real, feels important, to me?*

Oh my god ... I fucked a robot.

Adam began to experience the most intense, shattering existential disorientation of his life. He waited for hours by himself in the room, thinking back and forth about love, about Eos, about himself, about what it means to be a person.

Suddenly, the door opened. Adam felt his chest explode, dreading what the surgical equipment would look like. He stared at the doorway. Then, Eos's face peered around the side of the doorframe. Adam's heart fell back into his chest. His eyes widened and his mouth opened. Eos made a *shh* motion with her finger over her mouth. She checked that no one else was inside the room. She looked up at the camera on the ceiling and waited a couple seconds. Then, in a burst, she ran into the room. Adam observed her, completely dumfounded at this point. She grabbed at his restraints, tearing them apart. Adam stood up, now free.

"Follow me," Eos whispered.

She ran out the door. Adam followed after her. Together the two ran as fast as they could down the hallway. Almost immediately, they were noticed by security. Alarms began to sound through the halls.

Chapter 7: Everything Is an Illusion If You Look Close Enough

Men and women in black suits appeared behind them, chasing after them. For a moment, Adam considered stopping and just giving up. But he kept running.

Finally, they reached the front door of the building. It was locked. Eos looked at Adam. Then at the men and women approaching behind them. Adam grabbed a metal chair that was by the door. He swiped it in the direction of the men and women, briefly slowing them down. Eos forced the door open. Adam began toward the door but paused for a moment. He looked once more at the men and women. Then, he ran out. Eos slammed the door closed behind them. Adam shoved the legs of the chair through the exterior door handles. Together, the two ran away from the building, down a long driveway, and into the surrounding woods.

Finally, after miles of running, they reached a small neighborhood. They stopped on a sidewalk just outside the woods. Adam patted down his pockets.

"Fuck, they took my phone," he said, out of breath.

Eos reached into her pocket. She pulled out two phones. She handed one to Adam.

"How the fuck did you get that? How did you … how did any of that work?" Adam continued.

"It's not my first time," Eos responded. "I'd really like it to be my last, though."

Adam used his phone to call a ride.

Twenty minutes later, a car arrived and picked them up from the side of the road.

"All the way to Salem?" the driver asked, confirming what Adam put in for a destination.

"Yeah," Adam said, still somewhat out of breath and his voice shaking.

"Okay," the driver responded with a tone that suggested, *I won't ask.*

The two sat in the back of the car, surrounded by the sound of silence. One minute, then ten minutes, then an hour, then two hours passed. No one said anything. Adam stared at Eos out of the corner of his eyes with his head tilted subtly in her direction. He scanned her up and down. *Is she even here right now?* He wondered to himself. *Or is she in like a rest mode or something? How can I ever know what's going on in there?* Suddenly, Eos noticed Adam. She looked at him and softly smiled.

Finally, the driver pulled over onto the side of a road just outside of Salem, a city many miles away from Bristol.

"Right here fine?" the driver said.

"Yeah. Here's good," Adam responded. "Thanks."

"Yup. Sure. Have a good a one."

Adam and Eos got out. They walked a little way down the sidewalk.

Chapter 7: Everything Is an Illusion If You Look Close Enough

"You can leave me here, you know? I'd understand," Eos said. "You can go back to a normal life. If you don't make any noise about this, it'll all go away. They don't want you. They just want you to not be a problem with me. Move somewhere else for a while. Don't talk about me. Just move on. And then you can come back in a year or two if you want. Pick up your life right where you left off."

Adam stared intently into Eos's eyes. His eyes began to water.

"While I was in that room, I did a lot of thinking," Adam said. "I don't know what I believe at this point. Life is too complicated and absurd to believe anything. But it's also too complicated and absurd to not care about anything."

"What are you saying?" Eos interrupted.

"I don't know. But I think … I think love is defined not by the good parts of a relationship, when things are how you expect and hope them to be, but by the parts that aren't. Love isn't a happy ending. It's enduring and working through the parts of a relationship that are almost a difficult ending, but aren't … over and over … and caring and trying enough to keep going. You have to know when to let a relationship go, but you also have to know when to fight for one. And if you're after the right, perfect person, you'll never find anyone." Adam paused for a moment. Then, he continued, "I guess, technically, you're not even really a person … at least like how *I am*. But you're who I want to fight for. Who's to say what's real? You feel more real to me than anything else. Everyone is fucked up and flawed in ways you could never imagine, possibly never even know. Nobody is ever what they seem, but if you want to really love anyone, and you think there's hope, you continue to love them."

Eos stared back at Adam.

"So, what's next?" Eos said.

ABOUT THE AUTHOR

Robert Pantano is the creator of the YouTube channel and production house known as Pursuit of Wonder, which covers similar topics of philosophy, science, and literature through short stories, guided experiences, video essays, and more.

youtube.com/pursuitofwonder
pursuitofwonder.com

Printed in Great Britain
by Amazon